TABLE OF CONTENTS

TEXT EVIDENCE

RESTATE THE QUESTION.

This shows you understand what's being asked of you.

ANSWER THE QUESTION.

Share your opinion or background knowkedge about a topic.

PROVE YOU ARE RIGHT.

use text evidence to back up your writing.

TEXT EVIDENCE

RESTATE THE QUESTION.

Re-word the question into a statement.

ANSWER THE QUESTION.

What is being asked? Answer ALL parts of the question.

CITE TEXT EVIDENCE.

Tell where you found examples in the text. The author said... The text states...

EXPLAIN

Use evidence from the text to show your thinking. For Example... This shows...

TEXT EVIDENCE

R ESTATE THE QUESTION.

Re-word the question into a statement.

A NSWER THE QUESTION.

What is being asked? Answer ALL parts of the question.

C ITE TEXT EVIDENCE.

Tell where you found examples in the text. The author said... The text states...

E XPLAIN

Use evidence from the text to show your thinking. For Example... This shows...

TEXT EVIDENCE

ANSWER THE QUESTION.

using prior knowledge
and inferences..

CITE TEXT EVIDENCE.

evidence to support your
thoughts & opinions

EXPLAIN

your answer with evidence by
paraphrasing or directly quoting.

ON PAGE ____ IT SAID...

THE AUTHOR WROTE...

ACCORDING TO THE TEXT...

FROM THE READING, I KNOW...

AFTER I READ, I CONCLUDE...

I KNOW _____ BECAUSE...

FROM THE READING, I KNOW...

AFTER I READ, I CONCLUDE...

I KNOW ___ BECAUSE...

CREATE YOUR OWN FABLE

Fill in this plan to begin to think about your fable.

WHAT LESSON OR MORAL WOULD YOU LIKE TO TEACH?	
WHO WILL YOUR CHARACTERS BE? WILL THEY BE ANIMALS OR HUMANS?	
WHAT IS THE SETTING FOR YOUR FABLE?	
WHAT PROBLEM WILL YOUR CHARACTERS FACE?	
WHAT WILL THE SOLUTION BE? HOW WILL THE PROBLEM BE SOLVED?	
BEGINNING	
MIDDLE	
END	

GIVE YOUR FABLE A TITLE:

Name _____

CREATE YOUR OWN FABLE

Fill in this plan to begin to think about your fable.

WHAT LESSON OR MORAL WOULD YOU LIKE TO TEACH?	→
WHO WILL YOUR CHARACTERS BE? WILL THEY BE ANIMALS OR HUMANS?	→
WHAT IS THE SETTING FOR YOUR FABLE?	→
WHAT PROBLEM WILL YOUR CHARACTERS FACE?	→
WHAT WILL THE SOLUTION BE? HOW WILL THE PROBLEM BE SOLVED?	→
BEGINNING	→
MIDDLE	→
END	→

GIVE YOUR FABLE A TITLE:

Name _____

CREATE YOUR OWN FABLE

Fill in this plan to begin to think about your fable.

WHAT LESSON OR MORAL WOULD YOU LIKE TO TEACH?	→
WHO WILL YOUR CHARACTERS BE? WILL THEY BE ANIMALS OR HUMANS?	→
WHAT IS THE SETTING FOR YOUR FABLE?	→
WHAT PROBLEM WILL YOUR CHARACTERS FACE?	→
WHAT WILL THE SOLUTION BE? HOW WILL THE PROBLEM BE SOLVED?	→
BEGINNING	→
MIDDLE	→
END	→

GIVE YOUR FABLE A TITLE:

TEACHING WITH FABLES

THE FOX & THE STORK

THE FOX & THE STORK

The Fox one day thought of a plan to amuse himself at the expense of the Stork, at whose odd appearance he was always laughing. "You must come and dine with me today," he said to the Stork, smiling to himself at the trick he was going to play. The Stork gladly accepted the invitation and arrived in good time and with a very good appetite.

For dinner the Fox served soup. But it was set out in a very shallow dish, and all the Stork could do was to wet the very tip of his bill. Not a drop of soup could he get. But the Fox lapped it up easily, and, to increase the disappointment of the Stork, made a great show of enjoyment.

The hungry Stork was much displeased at the trick, but he was a calm, even-tempered fellow and saw no good in flying into a rage. Instead, not long afterward, he invited the Fox to dine with him in turn. The Fox arrived promptly at the time that had been set, and the Stork served a fish dinner that had a very appetizing smell. But it was served in a tall jar with a very narrow neck. The Stork could easily get at the food with his long bill, but all the Fox could do was to lick the outside of the jar, and sniff at the delicious odor. And when the Fox lost his temper, the Stork said calmly:

DO NOT PLAY TRICKS ON YOUR NEIGHBORS UNLESS YOU CAN STAND THE SAME TREATMENT YOURSELF.

THE FOX & THE STORK

The Fox one day thought of a plan to amuse himself at the expense of the Stork, at whose odd appearance he was always laughing. "You must come and dine with me today," he said to the Stork, smiling to himself at the trick he was going to play. The Stork gladly accepted the invitation and arrived in good time and with a very good appetite.

For dinner the Fox served soup. But it was set out in a very shallow dish, and all the Stork could do was to wet the very tip of his bill. Not a drop of soup could he get. But the Fox lapped it up easily, and, to increase the disappointment of the Stork, made a great show of enjoyment.

The hungry Stork was much displeased at the trick, but he was a calm, even-tempered fellow and saw no good in flying into a rage. Instead, not long afterward, he invited the Fox to dine with him in turn. The Fox arrived promptly at the time that had been set, and the Stork served a fish dinner that had a very appetizing smell. But it was served in a tall jar with a very narrow neck. The Stork could easily get at the food with his long bill, but all the Fox could do was to lick the outside of the jar, and sniff at the delicious odor. And when the Fox lost his temper, the Stork said calmly:

DO NOT PLAY TRICKS ON YOUR NEIGHBORS UNLESS YOU CAN STAND THE SAME TREATMENT YOURSELF.

DO NOT PLAY TRICKS ON SOMEONE UNLESS YOU CAN STAND THE SAME TREATMENT YOURSELF.

THE FOX & THE STORK
TEXT EVIDENCE

Underline the sentence with the color indicated on the crayon.

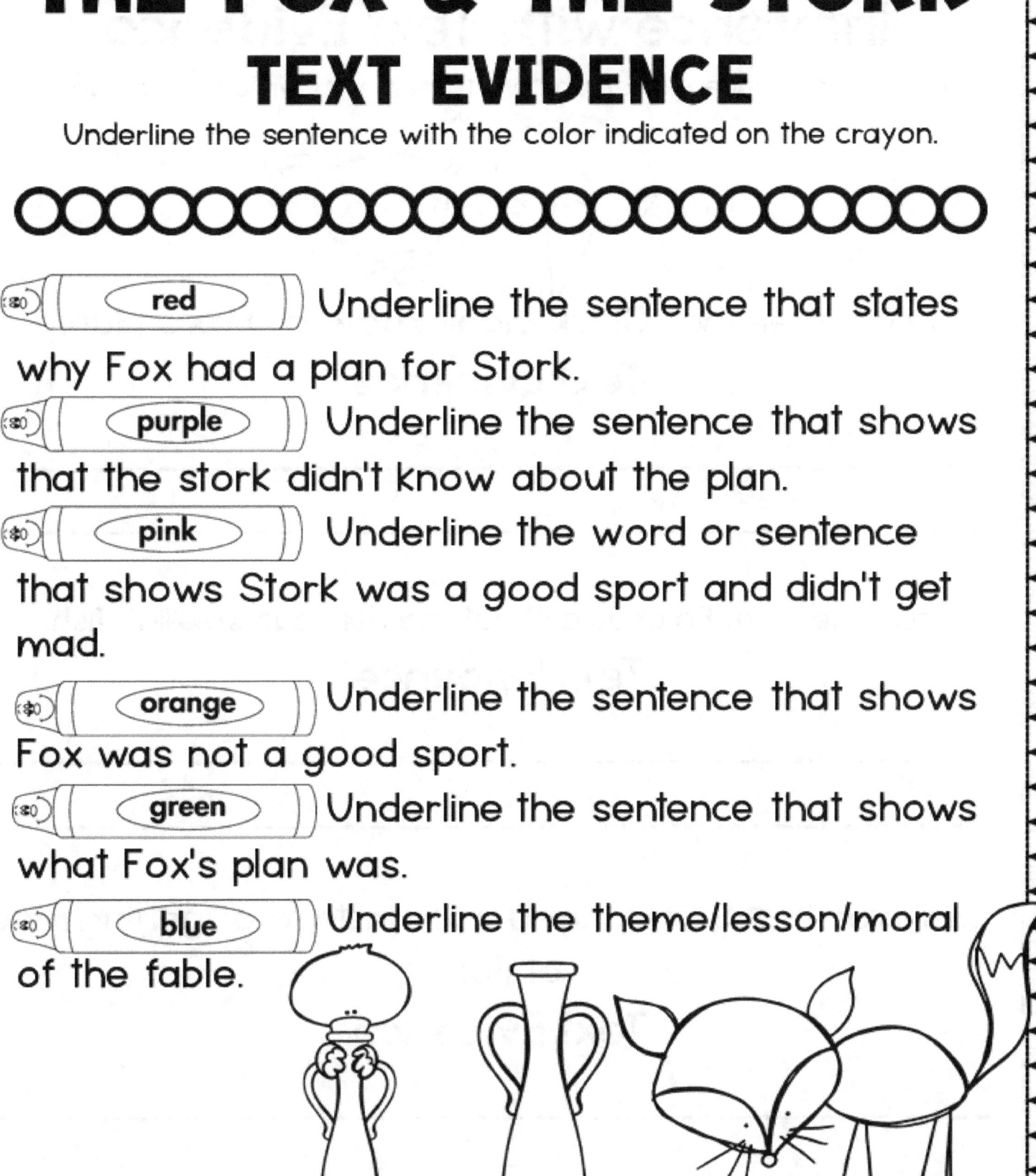

red — Underline the sentence that states why Fox had a plan for Stork.

purple — Underline the sentence that shows that the stork didn't know about the plan.

pink — Underline the word or sentence that shows Stork was a good sport and didn't get mad.

orange — Underline the sentence that shows Fox was not a good sport.

green — Underline the sentence that shows what Fox's plan was.

blue — Underline the theme/lesson/moral of the fable.

THE FOX & THE STORK
Inference with Text Evidence

Use the sentence starter posters to help you write you answers

I can infer that Stork didn't know of Fox's plan.

Text Evidence

_____

_____

I can infer that Fox couldn't eat the delicious smelling fish.

Text Evidence

_____

_____

I can infer that Stork stayed calm instead of getting mad at Fox.

Text Evidence

_____

_____

Name _____

THE FOX & THE STORK

CHARACTERS

SETTING

TITLE

PROBLEM

SOLUTION

THEME

Name _____

THE FOX & THE STORK

The moral or lesson of this fable is... _____

_____

_____

_____

FAVORITE CHARACTER

WHY?

Here is the evidence to support the moral or lesson...

_____

_____

_____

THE FOX & THE STORK

Write out what happened in your own words.

BEGINNING _____

_____

MIDDLE _____

_____

END _____

_____

THE FOX & THE STORK

○ Write a summary of the fable.

○ **SOMEBODY**

_____

○ **WANTED**

_____

○ **BUT**

_____

○ **SO**

_____

○ **THEN**

_____

The FOX and the STORK

The FOX and the STORK

The Fox one day thought of a plan to amuse himself at the expense of the Stork, at whose odd appearance he was always laughing.

The Fox one day thought of a plan to amuse himself at the expense of the Stork, at whose odd appearance he was always laughing.

"You must come and dine with me today," he said to the Stork, smiling to himself at the trick he was going to play. The Stork gladly accepted the invitation and arrived in good time and with a very good appetite.

"You must come and dine with me today," he said to the Stork, smiling to himself at the trick he was going to play. The Stork gladly accepted the invitation and arrived in good time and with a very good appetite.

"For dinner the Fox served soup. But it was set out in a very shallow dish, and all the Stork could do was to wet the very tip of his bill. Not a drop of soup could he get. But the Fox lapped it up easily, and, to increase the disappointment of the Stork, made a great show of enjoyment.

"For dinner the Fox served soup. But it was set out in a very shallow dish, and all the Stork could do was to wet the very tip of his bill. Not a drop of soup could he get. But the Fox lapped it up easily, and, to increase the disappointment of the Stork, made a great show of enjoyment.

The hungry Stork was much displeased at the trick, but he was a calm, even-tempered fellow and saw no good in flying into a rage. Instead, not long afterward, he invited the Fox to dine with him in turn.

" The hungry Stork was much displeased at the trick, but he was a calm, even-tempered fellow and saw no good in flying into a rage. Instead, not long afterward, he invited the Fox to dine with him in turn.

The Fox arrived promptly at the time that had been set, and the Stork served a fish dinner that had a very appetizing smell. But it was served in a tall jar with a very narrow neck. The Stork could easily get at the food with his long bill, but all the Fox could do was to lick the outside of the jar, and sniff at the delicious odor. And when the Fox lost his temper, the Stork said calmly:

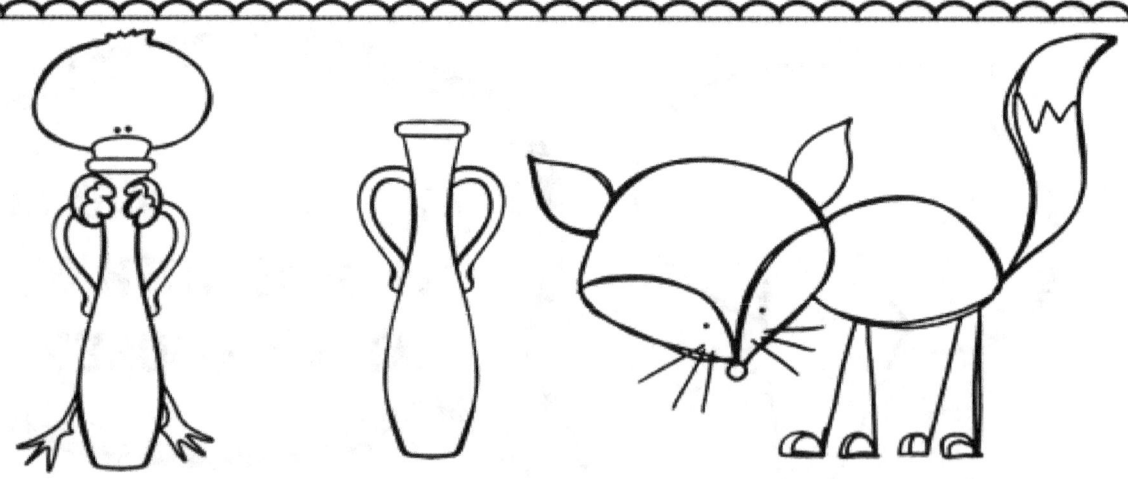

The Fox arrived promptly at the time that had been set, and the Stork served a fish dinner that had a very appetizing smell. But it was served in a tall jar with a very narrow neck. The Stork could easily get at the food with his long bill, but all the Fox could do was to lick the outside of the jar, and sniff at the delicious odor. And when the Fox lost his temper, the Stork said calmly:

DO NOT PLAY TRICKS ON YOUR NEIGHBORS UNLESS YOU CAN STAND THE SAME TREATMENT YOURSELF.

DO NOT PLAY TRICKS ON YOUR NEIGHBORS UNLESS YOU CAN STAND THE SAME TREATMENT YOURSELF.

TEACHING WITH FABLES

THE MILLER, DONKEY, & THEIR SON

Name _____

THE MILLER, HIS SON, & THE DONKEY

CHARACTERS

SETTING

TITLE

PROBLEM

SOLUTION

THEME

Name _____

THE MILLER, HIS SON, & THE DONKEY

The moral or lesson of this fable is... _____

_____

_____

_____

FAVORITE CHARACTER

WHY?

Here is the evidence to support the moral or lesson... _____

_____

_____

Name _____

THE MILLER, HIS SON, & THE DONKEY

Write out what happened in your own words.

BEGINNING

_____

_____

MIDDLE

_____

_____

END

_____

_____

Name _____

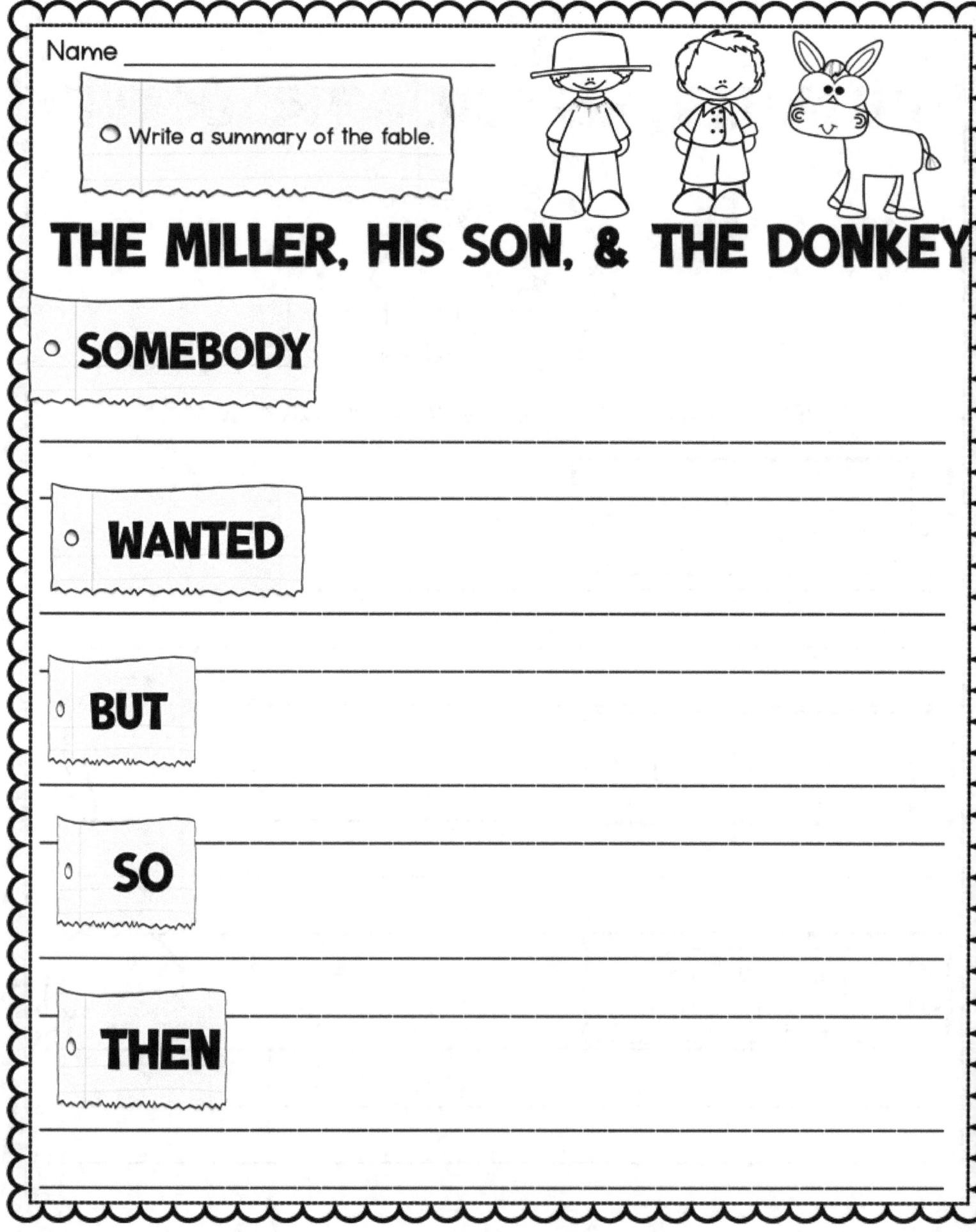

○ Write a summary of the fable.

THE MILLER, HIS SON, & THE DONKEY

○ **SOMEBODY**

_____

○ **WANTED**

_____

○ **BUT**

_____

○ **SO**

_____

○ **THEN**

_____

IF YOU TRY TO PLEASE ALL, YOU END UP PLEASING NONE!

THE MILLER, HIS SON, & THE DONKEY

They had no sooner started out again than a loud shout went up from another company of people on the road.

"What a crime," cried one, "to load up a poor dumb beast like that! They look more able to carry the poor creature, than he to carry them."

"They must be on their way to sell the poor thing's hide," said another.

The Miller and his Son quickly scrambled down, and a short time later, the marketplace was thrown into an uproar as the two came along carrying the Donkey slung from a pole. A great crowd of people ran out to get a closer look at the strange sight.

The Donkey did not dislike being carried, but so many people came up to point at him and laugh and shout, that he began to kick and bray, and then, just as they were crossing a bridge, the ropes that held him gave way, and down he tumbled into the river.

The poor Miller now set out sadly for home. By trying to please everybody, he had pleased nobody, and lost his Donkey in the end.

IF YOU TRY TO PLEASE ALL, YOU END UP PLEASING NONE!

THE MILLER, HIS SON, & THE DONKEY

They had no sooner started out again than a loud shout went up from another company of people on the road.

"What a crime," cried one, "to load up a poor dumb beast like that! They look more able to carry the poor creature, than he to carry them."

"They must be on their way to sell the poor thing's hide," said another.

The Miller and his Son quickly scrambled down, and a short time later, the marketplace was thrown into an uproar as the two came along carrying the Donkey slung from a pole. A great crowd of people ran out to get a closer look at the strange sight.

The Donkey did not dislike being carried, but so many people came up to point at him and laugh and shout, that he began to kick and bray, and then, just as they were crossing a bridge, the ropes that held him gave way, and down he tumbled into the river.

The poor Miller now set out sadly for home. By trying to please everybody, he had pleased nobody, and lost his Donkey in the end.

IF YOU TRY TO PLEASE ALL, YOU END UP PLEASING NONE!

THE MILLER, HIS SON, & THE DONKEY
Text Evidence

Underline the sentence with the color indicated on the crayon.

red — Underline the sentence that shows why Lion and Bull were at the same place.

purple — Underline the sentence which shows why Lion and Boar argued.

pink — Underline the sentence shows why Lion and Boar were so thirsty.

orange — Underline the sentence that shows why the Vultures were watching the fight.

green — Underline the word that means the same as fight.

blue — Underline the theme or lesson or moral of the story/fable.

Name _____

THE MILLER, HIS SON, & THE DONKEY
Inference with Text Evidence

Use the sentence starter posters to help you write you answers

I can infer that Lion and Boar must have been extremely thirsty

Text Evidence

_____

_____

I can infer that the Vultures wanted to eat the loser of the fight.

Text Evidence

_____

_____

I can infer that Lion and Boar were competitive with each other.

Text Evidence

_____

_____

THE MILLER
HIS SON
and their
DONKEY

THE MILLER
HIS SON
and their
DONKEY

One day, a long time ago, an old Miller and his Son were on
their way to market with a Donkey which they hoped to sell.
They drove him very slowly, for they thought they would have
a better chance to sell him if they kept him in good condition.

One day, a long time ago, an old Miller and his Son were on
their way to market with a Donkey which they hoped to sell.
They drove him very slowly, for they thought they would have
a better chance to sell him if they kept him in good condition.

As they walked along the highway some travelers laughed loudly at them. "What foolishness," cried one, "to walk when they might as well ride. The most stupid of the three is not the one you would expect it to be." The Miller did not like to be laughed at, so he told his son to climb up and ride.

As they walked along the highway some travelers laughed loudly at them. "What foolishness," cried one, "to walk when they might as well ride. The most stupid of the three is not the one you would expect it to be." The Miller did not like to be laughed at, so he told his son to climb up and ride.

They had gone a little farther along the road, when three merchants passed by. "Oh no, what have we here?" they cried. "Respect old age, young man! Get down and let the old man ride." Though the Miller was not tired, he made the boy get down and climbed up himself to ride, just to please the Merchants.

They had gone a little farther along the road, when three merchants passed by. "Oh no, what have we here?" they cried. "Respect old age, young man! Get down and let the old man ride." Though the Miller was not tired, he made the boy get down and climbed up himself to ride, just to please the Merchants.

At the next turnstile they overtook some women carrying market baskets loaded with vegetables and other things to sell.
"Look at the old fool," exclaimed one of them. "Perched on the Donkey, while that poor boy has to walk."
The Miller felt a bit confused....but to be agreeable he told the Boy to climb up behind him.

At the next turnstile they overtook some women carrying market baskets loaded with vegetables and other things to sell.
"Look at the old fool," exclaimed one of them. "Perched on the Donkey, while that poor boy has to walk."
The Miller felt a bit confused....but to be agreeable he told the Boy to climb up behind him.

They had no sooner started out again than a loud shout went up from another company of people on the road.
"What a crime," cried one, "to load up a poor dumb beast like that! They look more able to carry the poor creature, than he to carry them." "They must be on their way to sell the poor thing's hide," said another.

They had no sooner started out again than a loud shout went up from another company of people on the road.
"What a crime," cried one, "to load up a poor dumb beast like that! They look more able to carry the poor creature, than he to carry them." "They must be on their way to sell the poor thing's hide," said another.

The Miller and his Son quickly scrambled down, and a short time later, the marketplace was thrown into an uproar as the two came along carrying the Donkey slung from a pole. A great crowd of people ran out to get a closer look at the strange sight.

The Miller and his Son quickly scrambled down, and a short time later, the marketplace was thrown into an uproar as the two came along carrying the Donkey slung from a pole. A great crowd of people ran out to get a closer look at the strange sight.

The Donkey did not dislike being carried, but so many people came up to point at him and laugh and shout, that he began to kick and bray, and then, just as they were crossing a bridge, the ropes that held him gave way, and down he tumbled into the river. The poor Miller now set out sadly for home. By trying to please everybody, he had pleased nobody, and lost his Donkey in the end.

The Donkey did not dislike being carried, but so many people came up to point at him and laugh and shout, that he began to kick and bray, and then, just as they were crossing a bridge, the ropes that held him gave way, and down he tumbled into the river. The poor Miller now set out sadly for home. By trying to please everybody, he had pleased nobody, and lost his Donkey in the end.

IF YOU TRY TO PLEASE ALL, YOU END UP PLEASING NONE!

IF YOU TRY TO PLEASE ALL, YOU END UP PLEASING NONE!

TEACHING WITH FABLES

THE LION &
THE BOAR

THE LION & THE BOAR

On a summer day, when the great heat induced a general thirst, a Lion and a Boar came at the same moment to a small well to drink.

Lion and Boar fiercely argued which of them should drink first and were soon engaged in a big fight.

Stopping suddenly to take a breath, they saw some Vultures waiting in the distance to feast on the one which should "lose the fight."

They, at once, stopped their quarrel and said:

COOPERATION & UNITY CAN HELP INDIVIDUALS THRIVE, ESPECIALLY WHEN FACED WITH A COMMON ENEMY

UNITY IN THE FACE OF DANGER

THE LION & THE BOAR

On a summer day, when the great heat induced a general thirst, a Lion and a Boar came at the same moment to a small well to drink.

Lion and Boar fiercely argued which of them should drink first and were soon engaged in a big fight.

Stopping suddenly to take a breath, they saw some Vultures waiting in the distance to feast on the one which should "lose the fight."

They, at once, stopped their quarrel and said:

COOPERATION & UNITY CAN HELP INDIVIDUALS THRIVE, ESPECIALLY WHEN FACED WITH A COMMON ENEMY

Name _____

THE LION & THE BOAR
Text Evidence

◯◯◯◯◯◯◯◯◯◯◯◯◯◯◯◯◯◯◯◯◯◯◯◯

red Underline the sentence that shows why Lion and Bull were at the same place.

purple Underline the sentence which shows why Lion and Boar argued.

pink Underline the sentence shows why Lion and Boar were so thirsty.

orange Underline the sentence that shows why the Vultures were watching the fight.

green Underline the word that means the same as fight.

blue Underline the theme or lesson or moral of the story/fable.

THE LION & THE BOAR
Inference with Text Evidence

Use the sentence starter posters to help you write you answers

I can infer that Lion and Boar must have been extremely thirsty.

Text Evidence

_____

_____

I can infer that the Vultures wanted to eat the loser of the fight.

Text Evidence

_____

_____

I can infer that Lion and Boar were competitive with each other.

Text Evidence

_____

_____

On a summer day, when the great heat induced a general thirst, a Lion and a Boar came at the same moment to a small well to drink.

On a summer day, when the great heat induced a general thirst, a Lion and a Boar came at the same moment to a small well to drink.

Lion and Boar fiercely argued which of them should drink first and were soon engaged in a big fight.

Lion and Boar fiercely argued which of them should drink first and were soon engaged in a big fight.

Stopping suddenly to take a breath, they saw some
Vultures waiting in the distance to feast on the one
which should "lose the fight."

Stopping suddenly to take a breath, they saw some
Vultures waiting in the distance to feast on the one
which should "lose the fight."

They, at once, stopped their quarrel and said:

They, at once, stopped their quarrel and said:

UNITY IN THE FACE OF DANGER:

cooperation and unity can help individuals survive and thrive, especially when faced with a common enemy.

UNITY IN THE FACE OF DANGER:

cooperation and unity can help individuals survive and thrive, especially when faced with a common enemy.

Name _____

THE LION & THE BOAR

CHARACTERS

SETTING

TITLE

PROBLEM

SOLUTION

THEME

Name _____

THE LION & THE BOAR

The moral or lesson of this fable is... _____

_____

_____

_____

FAVORITE CHARACTER

WHY?

Here is the evidence to support the moral or lesson... _____

_____

_____

_____

Name _____

THE LION & THE BOAR

Write out what happened in your own words.

BEGINNING

_____

_____

MIDDLE

_____

_____

END

_____

_____

Name _____

THE LION & THE BOAR

○ Write a summary of the fable.

○ **SOMEBODY**

_____

○ **WANTED**

_____

○ **BUT**

_____

○ **SO**

_____

○ **THEN**

_____

_____

TEACHING WITH FABLES

THE ANT & THE DOVE

THE ANT & THE DOVE

A Dove saw an Ant fall into river. The Ant struggled in vain to reach the bank, so in pity, the Dove dropped a blade of straw close beside it.

Clinging to the straw like a shipwrecked sailor, the Ant floated safely to shore.

Soon after, the Ant saw a man getting ready to kill the Dove with a stone. But just as he cast the stone, the Ant stung him in the heel, so that the pain made him miss his aim, and the startled Dove flew to safety in a distant wood.

KINDNESS IS NEVER WASTED.

THE ANT & THE DOVE

A Dove saw an Ant fall into river. The Ant struggled in vain to reach the bank, so in pity, the Dove dropped a blade of straw close beside it.

Clinging to the straw like a shipwrecked sailor, the Ant floated safely to shore.

Soon after, the Ant saw a man getting ready to kill the Dove with a stone. But just as he cast the stone, the Ant stung him in the heel, so that the pain made him miss his aim, and the startled Dove flew to safety in a distant wood.

KINDNESS IS NEVER WASTED.

THE ANT & THE DOVE

Text Evidence

Underline the sentence with the color indicated on the crayon.

red) Underline the sentence that shows what happens to Ant in the beginning.

purple) Underline the sentence that shows what the dove did to save Ant.

pink) Underline the sentence that is a metaphor.

orange) Underline the sentence that shows what the man tries to do to Dove.

green) Underline the sentence that shows how Ant saved Dove.

blue) Underline the theme of the fable.

THE ANT & THE DOVE

Inference with Text Evidence

Use the sentence starter posters to help you write you answers

I can infer that Dove felt sorry for Ant.

Text Evidence

_____

I can infer that Ant was grateful to Dove for saving him.

Text Evidence

_____

I can infer that Ant was paying back Dove for saving him.

Text Evidence

_____

The ANT & the _____ DOVE

The ANT & the _____ DOVE

A Dove saw an Ant fall into river. The Ant struggled in vain to reach the bank, so in pity, the Dove dropped a blade of straw close beside it.

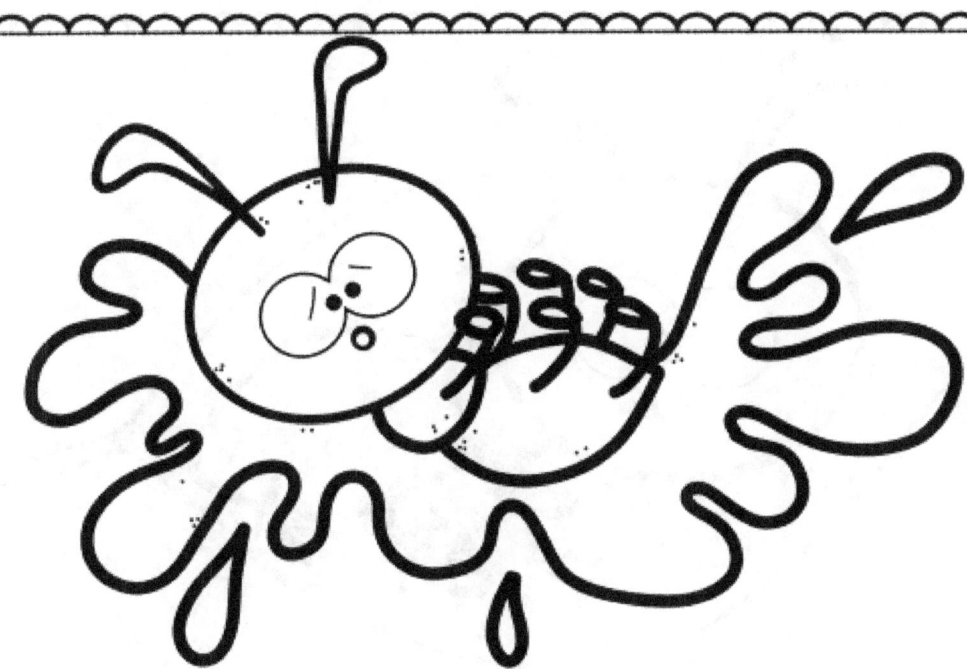

A Dove saw an Ant fall into river. The Ant struggled in vain to reach the bank, so in pity, the Dove dropped a blade of straw close beside it.

Clinging to the straw like a shipwrecked sailor, the Ant floated safely to shore.

Clinging to the straw like a shipwrecked sailor, the Ant floated safely to shore.

Soon after, the Ant saw a man getting ready to kill the Dove with a stone.

Soon after, the Ant saw a man getting ready to kill the Dove with a stone.

But just as he cast the stone, the Ant stung him in the heel, so that the pain made him miss his aim, and the startled Dove flew to safety in a distant wood.

But just as he cast the stone, the Ant stung him in the heel, so that the pain made him miss his aim, and the startled Dove flew to safety in a distant wood.

KINDNESS IS NEVER WASTED.

KINDNESS IS NEVER WASTED.

Name _____

THE ANT & THE DOVE

CHARACTERS

SETTING

TITLE

PROBLEM

SOLUTION

THEME

Name _____

THE ANT & THE DOVE

The moral or lesson of this fable is... _____

_____

_____

_____

FAVORITE CHARACTER

WHY?

Here is the evidence to support the moral or lesson... _____

_____

_____

_____

Name _____

THE ANT & THE DOVE

Write out what happened in your own words.

BEGINNING

_____

_____

MIDDLE

_____

_____

END

_____

_____

THE ANT & THE DOVE

○ Write a summary of the fable.

○ **SOMEBODY**

_____

○ **WANTED**

_____

_____

○ **BUT**

_____

_____

○ **SO**

_____

_____

○ **THEN**

_____

_____

TEACHING WITH FABLES

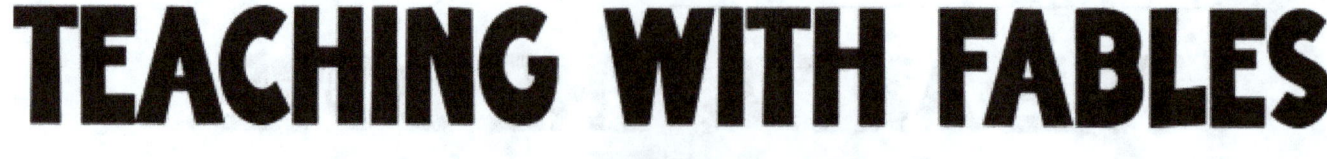

THE FOX & THE ROOSTER

DECEITFUL BEHAVIOR OFTEN LEADS TO NEGATIVE CONSEQUENCES.

THE FOX & THE ROOSTER

A Dog and a Rooster, who were the best of friends, wished very much to see something of the world. So they decided to leave the farmyard and to set out into the world along the road that led to the woods. The two comrades traveled along in the very best of spirits and without meeting any adventure to speak of. At nightfall the Rooster, looking for a place to roost, as was his custom, spied nearby a hollow tree that he thought would do very nicely for a night's lodging. The Dog could creep inside and the Rooster would fly up on one of the branches. So said, so done, and both slept very comfortably.

With the first glimmer of dawn the Rooster awoke. For the moment he forgot just where he was. He thought he was still in the farmyard where it had been his duty to arouse the household at daybreak. So standing on tip-toes he flapped his wings and crowed lustily. But instead of awakening the farmer, he awakened a Fox not far off in the wood. The Fox immediately had rosy visions of a very delicious breakfast. Hurrying to the tree where the Rooster was roosting, he said very politely:

"A hearty welcome to our woods, honored sir. I cannot tell you how glad I am to see you here. I am quite sure we shall become the closest of friends."

"I feel highly flattered, kind sir," replied the Rooster slyly. "If you will please go around to the door of my house at the foot of the tree, my porter will let you in."

The hungry but unsuspecting Fox, went around the tree as he was told, and in a twinkling the Dog had seized him.

THOSE WHO TRY TO DECEIVE MAY EXPECT TO BE PAID IN THEIR OWN COIN.

THE FOX & THE ROOSTER

A Dog and a Rooster, who were the best of friends, wished very much to see something of the world. So they decided to leave the farmyard and to set out into the world along the road that led to the woods. The two comrades traveled along in the very best of spirits and without meeting any adventure to speak of. At nightfall the Rooster, looking for a place to roost, as was his custom, spied nearby a hollow tree that he thought would do very nicely for a night's lodging. The Dog could creep inside and the Rooster would fly up on one of the branches. So said, so done, and both slept very comfortably.

With the first glimmer of dawn the Rooster awoke. For the moment he forgot just where he was. He thought he was still in the farmyard where it had been his duty to arouse the household at daybreak. So standing on tip-toes he flapped his wings and crowed lustily. But instead of awakening the farmer, he awakened a Fox not far off in the wood. The Fox immediately had rosy visions of a very delicious breakfast. Hurrying to the tree where the Rooster was roosting, he said very politely:

"A hearty welcome to our woods, honored sir. I cannot tell you how glad I am to see you here. I am quite sure we shall become the closest of friends."

"I feel highly flattered, kind sir," replied the Rooster slyly. "If you will please go around to the door of my house at the foot of the tree, my porter will let you in."

The hungry but unsuspecting Fox, went around the tree as he was told, and in a twinkling the Dog had seized him.

THOSE WHO TRY TO DECEIVE MAY EXPECT TO BE PAID IN THEIR OWN COIN.

Name _____

THE FOX & THE ROOSTER

Text Evidence

red Underline the word that means the same as friend.

purple Underline the sentence which shows why Rooster got up and crowed loudly.

pink Underline the sentence that shows Fox trying to deceive Rooster.

orange Underline the word or sentence that shows that the cows were angry with the dog.

green Underline the word that gives away the fact that Rooster knew Fox was playing a trick.

blue Underline the theme of the story/fable.

Name _____

THE FOX & THE ROOSTER
Inference with Text Evidence
Use the sentence starter posters to help you write you answers

I can infer that the Dog and Rooster are friends.
Text Evidence
_____
_____

I can infer that Fox was playing a trick on Rooster.
Text Evidence
_____
_____

I can infer that Rooster was playing a trick back on Fox.
Text Evidence
_____
_____

A Dog and a Rooster wished very much to see something of the world. So they decided to leave the farmyard and to set out into the world along the road that led to the woods. The two comrades traveled along in the very best of spirits and without meeting any adventure to speak of.

A Dog and a Rooster wished very much to see something of the world. So they decided to leave the farmyard and to set out into the world along the road that led to the woods. The two comrades traveled along in the very best of spirits and without meeting any adventure to speak of.

At nightfall the Rooster, looking for a place to roost, as was his custom, spied nearby a hollow tree that he thought would do very nicely for a night's lodging. The Dog could creep inside, and the Rooster would fly up on one of the branches. So said, so done, and both slept very comfortably.

At nightfall the Rooster, looking for a place to roost, as was his custom, spied nearby a hollow tree that he thought would do very nicely for a night's lodging. The Dog could creep inside, and the Rooster would fly up on one of the branches. So said, so done, and both slept very comfortably.

. But instead of awakening the farmer, he awakened a Fox not far off in the wood. The Fox immediately had rosy visions of a very delicious breakfast. Hurrying to the tree where the Rooster was roosting, he said very politely: "A hearty welcome to our woods, honored sir. I cannot tell you how glad I am to see you here. I am quite sure we shall become the closest of friends."

. But instead of awakening the farmer, he awakened a Fox not far off in the wood. The Fox immediately had rosy visions of a very delicious breakfast. Hurrying to the tree where the Rooster was roosting, he said very politely: "A hearty welcome to our woods, honored sir. I cannot tell you how glad I am to see you here. I am quite sure we shall become the closest of friends."

With the first glimmer of dawn the Rooster awoke. For the moment he forgot just where he was. He thought he was still in the farmyard where it had been his duty to arouse the household at daybreak. So, standing on tip-toes he flapped his wings and crowed lustily.

With the first glimmer of dawn the Rooster awoke. For the moment he forgot just where he was. He thought he was still in the farmyard where it had been his duty to arouse the household at daybreak. So, standing on tip-toes he flapped his wings and crowed lustily.

THOSE WHO TRY TO DECEIVE MAY
EXPECT TO BE PAID IN RETURN.

THOSE WHO TRY TO DECEIVE MAY
EXPECT TO BE PAID IN RETURN.

Name _____

THE FOX & THE ROOSTER

CHARACTERS

SETTING

TITLE

PROBLEM

SOLUTION

THEME

Name _____

THE FOX & THE ROOSTER

The moral or lesson of this fable is... _____

_____

_____

_____

FAVORITE CHARACTER

WHY?

Here is the evidence to support the moral or lesson... _____

_____

_____

_____

THE FOX & THE ROOSTER

Write out what happened in your own words.

BEGINNING

_____

_____

MIDDLE

_____

_____

END

_____

_____

Name _____

THE FOX & THE ROOSTER

○ Write a summary of the fable.

○ **SOMEBODY**

_____

○ **WANTED**

_____

○ **BUT**

_____

○ **SO**

_____

○ **THEN**

_____

_____

TEACHING WITH FABLES

THE CROW & THE PITCHER

THE CROW & THE PITCHER

In a spell of dry weather, when the Birds could find very little to drink, a thirsty Crow found a pitcher with a little water in it. But the pitcher was high and had a narrow neck, and no matter how he tried, the Crow could not reach the water. The poor thing felt as if he must die of thirst.

Then an idea came to him. Picking up some small pebbles, he dropped them into the pitcher one by one. With each pebble the water rose a little higher until at last it was near enough so he could drink.

IN AN INSTANT, USE YOUR GOOD WIT TO HELP YOURSELF.

IN AN INSTANT, USE YOUR GOOD WIT TO HELP YOURSELF.

THE CROW & THE PITCHER

In a spell of dry weather, when the Birds could find very little to drink, a thirsty Crow found a pitcher with a little water in it. But the pitcher was high and had a narrow neck, and no matter how he tried, the Crow could not reach the water. The poor thing felt as if he must die of thirst.

Then an idea came to him. Picking up some small pebbles, he dropped them into the pitcher one by one. With each pebble the water rose a little higher until at last it was near enough so he could drink.

IN AN INSTANT, USE YOUR GOOD WIT TO HELP YOURSELF.

THE CROW & THE PITCHER

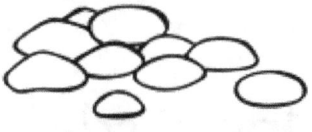

Text Evidence

Underline the sentence with the color indicated on the crayon.

red) Underline the sentence that shows why the Birds couldn't find any water.

purple) Underline the word that means the same as really wanting or needing something to drink.

pink) Underline the sentence that shows what might happen to the crow if he couldn't get a drink.

orange) Underline the sentence that shows the crow's good idea.

green) Underline the sentence that shows what adding the pebbles did to the water.

blue) Underline the theme of the fable.

THE CROW & THE PITCHER
Inference with Text Evidence

Use the sentence starter posters to help you write you answers

I can infer that the Birds were very thirsty.

Text Evidence

_____

_____

I can that Crow was probably frustrated when he couldn't reach the water.

Text Evidence

_____

_____

I can infer that Crow is very smart.

Text Evidence

_____

_____

The CROW and the PITCHER

The CROW and the PITCHER

In a spell of dry weather, when the Birds could find very little to drink, a thirsty Crow found a pitcher with a little water in it.

In a spell of dry weather, when the Birds could find very little to drink, a thirsty Crow found a pitcher with a little water in it.

But the pitcher was high and had a narrow neck, and no matter how he tried, the Crow could not reach the water. The poor thing felt as if he must die of thirst.

But the pitcher was high and had a narrow neck, and no matter how he tried, the Crow could not reach the water. The poor thing felt as if he must die of thirst.

Then an idea came to him. Picking up some small pebbles, he dropped them into the pitcher one by one. With each pebble the water rose a little higher until at last it was near enough so he could drink.

Then an idea came to him. Picking up some small pebbles, he dropped them into the pitcher one by one. With each pebble the water rose a little higher until at last it was near enough so he could drink.

IN AN INSTANT, USE YOUR GOOD WIT TO HELP YOURSELF.

IN AN INSTANT, USE YOUR GOOD WIT TO HELP YOURSELF.

Name _____

THE CROW & THE PITCHER

CHARACTERS

SETTING

TITLE

PROBLEM

SOLUTION

THEME

Name _____

THE CROW & THE PITCHER

The moral or lesson of this fable is... _____

_____

_____

_____

FAVORITE CHARACTER

WHY?

Here is the evidence to support the moral or lesson... _____

_____

_____

Name _____

THE CROW & THE PITCHER

Write out what happened in your own words.

BEGINNING

_____

_____

MIDDLE

_____

_____

END

_____

_____

Name _____

THE CROW & THE PITCHER

Write a summary of the fable.

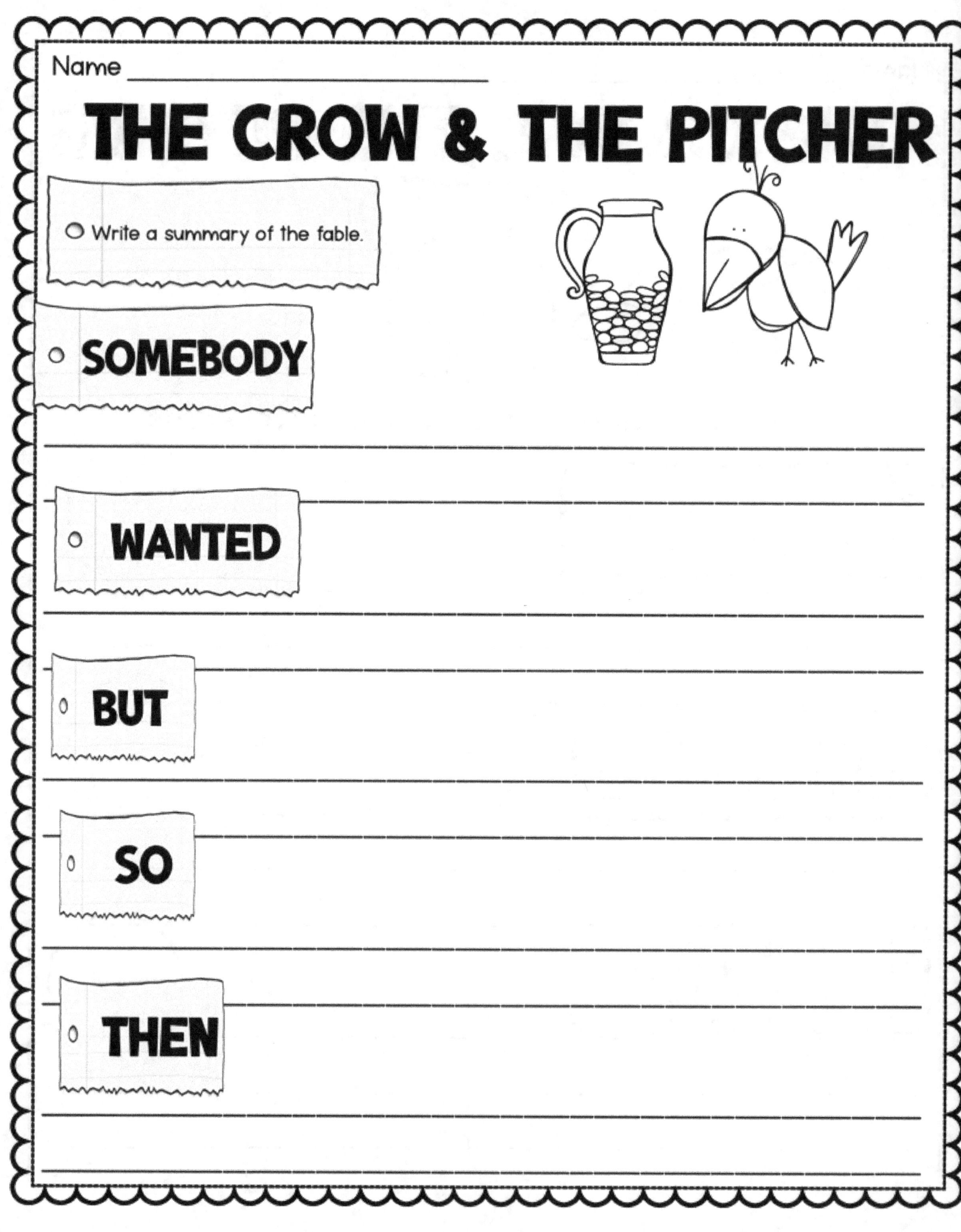

○ **SOMEBODY**

_____

○ **WANTED**

_____

○ **BUT**

_____

○ **SO**

_____

○ **THEN**

_____

TEACHING WITH FABLES

Stephani Ann

Graphics by...